ILLUSTRATED

The Invisible Man

H.G. Wells

Adapted by
Malvina G. Vogel

Published by Playmore Inc., Publishers and
Waldman Publishing Corp., New York, New York

ILLUSTRATED CLASSIC EDITIONS

Printed in Canada

Contents

About the Author

Herbert George Wells was born on September 21, 1866 in Kent, England, the youngest of three sons. His mother, a housemaid, began teaching her son to read at the age of three, and little "Bertie"—as his family called him, never stopped reading as he grew up. He read anything he could get his young hands on.

A broken leg at the age of 7 kept Bertie in bed for several months. To keep him occupied, his father brought home library books on astronomy, biology, and botany. This started Wells on a lifelong love of science, opening up to him worlds he had never seen or heard of. He later called that broken leg his "lucky moment" in life.

Bertie didn't have a good education because that cost money, and his father barely made a living. So, even though he was forced to leave school and go to work at the age of 14, his love of reading, his fascination with science, and his determination to teach himself resulted in a scholarship to the Royal College of Science in London when he was 18. After graduation, he began teaching science, and his first published work was a *Textbook of Biology*.

H.G. Wells wanted to spend his time writing. Even though he had read mainly non-fiction for years to gain what he called "useful knowledge," it was his fiction that brought him worldwide fame and wealth.

Wells used his knowledge of science and his imaginative genius to create his "scientific fantasies" that would take readers to possible future worlds in *The Time Machine* (1895), *The Island of Dr. Moreau* (1896), *The Invisible Man* (1897), *The War of the Worlds* (1898), and *The First Men in the Moon* (1901).

Struggling through the Storm

Chapter 1

A Mysterious Bandaged Stranger

It was a snowy February night when a stranger got off the train at Bramblehurst railway station in the southern part of England. A large-brimmed hat and long black coat covered him from head to foot, but they barely protected him from the biting wind and heavy snow that piled up on him and on the small black suitcase he was carrying in his gloved hands.

There were no carriages at the station, and the man was forced to struggle through the storm on foot for several hours to reach his destination—the small village of Iping.

Flinging open the door of the Coach and Horses Inn, the exhausted stranger staggered inside, more dead than alive. Keeping his head down on his chest, the man gasped, "A room and a fire! And hurry, please!"

"I'm Mrs. Hall, the innkeeper here," said a woman coming out from behind the bar. "If you'll just follow me upstairs, sir, I'll show you to a room."

The stranger kept his back to Mrs. Hall as they negotiated a price for his room and meals. Then, after lighting a fire in the fireplace for the man, Mrs. Hall went downstairs to prepare a meal for him.

By the time she returned with a tray of hot food, the fire was burning brightly, making the room warm and comfortable. The stranger, however, still wore his coat, hat, and gloves as he stood at the window, staring out at the storm.

"The snow from your coat and hat is melting

"A Room and a Fire!"

on my carpet, sir," said Mrs. Hall. "May I take them and dry them in the kitchen?"

"No!" snapped the man, finally turning to face her. "I prefer to keep them on."

At that moment, Mrs. Hall got her first real look at the man. Below the wide brim of the hat were big blue glasses that wrapped around the front and sides of his eyes. A bushy beard and sideburns came down over his coat collar, completely hiding his cheeks and chin.

"Very well," she said and left the room.

Upon her return to the kitchen, she discovered that she had forgotten the mustard for the man's meat, so she put it on a tray and went back upstairs with it.

She knocked once, then immediately opened the door. Her sudden appearance surprised the man, and all she saw was a flash of white as he ducked under the table.

"I suppose I can take these now, sir?" she asked, pointing to the overcoat and hat on a chair in front of the fire.

Her First Real Look at the Man

"The coat, yes, but leave the hat," came a muffled voice as the man sat up.

Mrs. Hall gaped in shock at the sight before her. Behind the blue glasses were masses of white bandages wrapped around the man's head. Only a shiny pink nose and thick patches of black hair stuck out between the bandages. Just as strange were his hands, still wearing gloves, as they held a large napkin over the lower part of his face, completely covering his mouth and jaw. His dark brown dressing gown had its high collar turned up and a scarf knotted at the front.

"Leave the hat," repeated the man firmly.

"Y-yes, sir," stammered the woman as she slowly began to recover from her shock. "I didn't know, sir, that—"

"Thank you, madam. That will be all."

Mrs. Hall picked up his coat and hurried out of the room, shivering as she closed the door behind her. "The poor soul's had an accident or operation or something," she muttered to her-

Gaping in Shock!

self. "What a scare those bandages gave me! And he must've hurt his mouth too, the way he was talkin' through the napkin. Poor soul!"

Once the stranger had finished his meal, he settled himself in an armchair in front of the fire and lit his pipe. Knowing that Mrs. Hall would be returning to pick up the tray, he wrapped the scarf loosely around the lower part of his face, leaving room for the stem of the pipe to reach his lips.

When the woman knocked and entered a while later, she found that the food and drink and warmth had changed the stranger's mood as he spoke to her more politely than before.

"I have some luggage at Bramblehurst station, Mrs. Hall. How can I have it brought here?"

"My husband will be back later tonight with our horse and cart. He can get it for you tomorrow."

"Isn't there anyone who can go tonight?"

"Not and risk an accident on the steep roads

Settling in an Armchair

in this weather. You surely know what accidents can—"

"Yes, I do. I, too, had an accident. It left my eyes weak, so I must stay in darkness and wear these glasses most days."

"What kind of acci—"

"That is not important, Mrs. Hall. All I can tell you is I'm a scientist working on a very crucial experiment. My baggage contains all my instruments, my chemicals, and my notebooks. I need to get to my work without any further delay. But if tomorrow is the earliest I can get it, that will have to do. Goodnight, madam."

Mrs. Hall left the room, muttering to herself, "Sensitive about accidents, ain't he!"

She couldn't wait to get back down to the bar to give her customers a vivid description of her mysterious guest.

Most of the men showed sympathy for the stranger because of his accident, except Teddy Henfrey, the village clockmaker.

"I'm a Scientist."

"Accident? Ha!" snapped Teddy. "He's got to be hiding out from the police. Wrapping himself up in all those bandages has to be the best way to hide."

"And who's hiding behind what bandages?" came a voice at the door to the inn.

"The stranger your wife just rented a room to, Mr. Hall," said Teddy. "I'd take a good look at his luggage when you bring it here from the station tomorrow."

"You mind your own business, Teddy!" snapped Mrs. Hall. "And you, too, Hall. This is my inn, and I'll run it as I see fit!"

But in spite of her strong words, Mrs. Hall had to admit to herself that she, too, was suspicious about the stranger. And those suspicions filled her dreams that night with huge black eyes in white turnip heads at the end of long necks . . . heads that were chasing her through the streets of the village!

"He's Hiding from the Police."

"Come Along with Those Things!"

Chapter 2

The Experiment Begins

The next morning when Mr. Hall drove his cart up to the inn, he called out for help in unloading the stranger's luggage.

"Good Heavens!" cried his wife as she came out. "I expected a few trunks to be put in his room, but he's got dozens of boxes, six wooden crates, and who knows what else!"

"Come along with those things!" called the stranger as he came out of the inn. "I've been waiting long enough." His coat collar was turned up, his wide-brimmed hat was pulled down over his face, and his hands were covered with his heavy dark gloves.

Just as he was about to lift one of the smaller crates from the cart, a neighborhood dog ran up to the stranger and sprang at his hand. Before Mr. Hall could reach into the cart for his whip, the dog's teeth let go of the stranger's gloved hand and clamped onto his trouser leg.

The next moment, the whip came down onto the dog's back, forcing him to release his bite on the trousers. As the Halls cursed and shouted at the dog's approaching owner, the stranger glanced at his torn glove and trousers, then hurried into the inn and up to his room.

"I'd better go in and see if he's all right," said Hall.

"Yes, and hurry," answered his wife.

Finding the stranger's door open, Hall entered the room, prepared to offer his sympathy and any help the man might need. The drapes were closed, making the room dim, and Hall saw the strangest thing—the arm of the man's

The Whip Came Down.

coat was waving at him...but without a hand! The next moment, Hall was struck hard in the chest, then pushed back out of the room and the door slammed in his face.

Hall stood outside the door, scratching his head in bewilderment. "What did I see in there? Did I see anything?"

He went back downstairs, still bewildered. By now, a crowd had gathered out front as his wife argued with the dog's owner, who was holding the animal by the collar.

Since Hall still didn't know what he had actually seen in the bedroom, he simply told his wife, "He didn't want any help. I think we'd better get his luggage up to him."

"You ought to have the doctor look at the bite," suggested one woman in the crowd.

"I didn't see any blood," said another, "or even any skin under the trousers or gloves when they tore."

"No matter," added a man. "Just shoot that dog and be done with it."

Without a Hand

Just then, the dog tried to pull away. He pointed his nose towards the inn and began growling. All eyes turned to the entrance.

"Come along, Hall!" cried an angry voice at the door. It was the stranger, wearing new trousers and waving with a fresh pair of gloves. His coat collar was still turned up, and his big hat was again pulled down over his face.

"Were you hurt, sir?" asked Mrs. Hall.

"Not a bit. He never broke the skin. Now, hurry up with those things, Mr. Hall."

No sooner had the crates been set down in the stranger's room than he eagerly flung himself down on them and began to unpack. He scattered straw from the crates all over the carpet as he took out assorted instruments and handwritten notebooks, along with scores of test tubes and bottles in all shapes, sizes, and colors. Some contained powders, others liquids, and still others were labeled *Poison*. He set them up on cabinets, shelves, bookcas-

Scores of Test Tubes

es, window ledges, and tables all over the room. It looked more like the village pharmacy than a bedroom.

The trunks of clothes and boxes of books were left untouched as the man began his experiments. He worked steadily all morning, pouring drops from bottles into test tubes, mixing and swirling them around with powder. He didn't even stop when Mrs. Hall knocked and came into the room with his lunch tray.

He paid no attention to her, but as she put the tray on the table, she noticed that he wasn't wearing his blue glasses.

"My Gawd!" she gasped under her breath. "His eye sockets look as if they're empty!"

The stranger heard the gasp and quickly put his glasses back on. "I wish you would not come in without knocking!" he snapped.

"I did knock, several times, sir, but you obviously didn't—"

"Yes, yes, perhaps you did. But my experi-

As If They're Empty!

ments require my complete concentration. I cannot have any disturbance at all."

"I understand, sir. There *is* a lock on the door. You can use it anytime you wish. Also, these piles of straw from your unpacking will mean extra clean—"

"Don't bother me with that. Put an extra charge on my bill. Now leave me to my work."

For the next several hours, no sounds came from the stranger's room as he worked in silence. Then suddenly, Mrs. Hall heard the smashing of bottles, followed by footsteps rapidly stomping around the room. Fearing that something terrible may have happened, she hurried up the stairs and listened at the door, afraid to knock.

"I can't go on like this!" she heard the man raving. "I *can't* go on! It may take me the rest of my life to find the answer to this experiment! I don't have the time! I don't have the patience! What am I to do?"

"I Can't Go On Like This!"

Scaring Children

Chapter 3

Feeling *Something*, But Seeing *Nothing*!

For the next two months, until the end of April, the stranger worked every day and most nights. He stopped occasionally to take walks, but only at twilight.

He always kept his face and hands covered when Mrs. Hall brought him his food or when he went outdoors. He ignored greetings from villagers on those walks and seemed to enjoy scaring children who teased him. He talked to himself behind locked doors and went into rages, smashing furniture and equipment.

When Mrs. Hall complained about her ruined furnishings, he paid her for the damage and always added something extra.

On several occasions, Mr. Hall asked his wife to get rid of the stranger, but each time, she reminded him, "This time of year we don't have many paying guests. I'll wait until the summer business starts. For now, he pays his bills and we can use the money."

During his three months in Iping, the stranger became a regular topic of conversation among the villagers. Questions about him were answered by Mrs. Hall with explanations such as, "He's an important scientist working on some very secret experiments for the government," or "He's had an accident which scarred his face and hands, and since he's a very sensitive gentleman, he doesn't care to be seen in public."

Many of the townspeople, however, preferred Teddy Henfrey's explanation that the man was a criminal trying to hide from the po-

A Regular Topic of Conversation

lice by wrapping himself up in bandages. Others didn't waste too much time on the man and simply decided he was a harmless lunatic.

One person in Iping was more curious about the stranger than most others. That was John Cuss, the village doctor, who was intrigued by the stories of the "thousands" of bottles in the man's room and wanted to see them. When he finally came up with a good reason for calling on the stranger—to request a donation to the Iping Nurse Fund, Dr. Cuss made his way to the Coach and Horses Inn.

Mrs. Hall led the doctor up the stairs and waited as he knocked at the door. A low voice muttered something in reply. Assuming that the reply was permission to enter, the doctor opened the door and went inside.

Mrs. Hall, however, didn't move from the hallway after Dr. Cuss had closed the door behind him. She was much too curious to leave, so she stood there for ten minutes. But all she heard was the murmur of voices.

The Doctor Went Inside.

Suddenly, a cry of surprise made her jump back. It was followed by the rapid shuffling of feet and a bark of laughter. Then the door burst open, and Dr. Cuss came running through it, his eyes staring back into the room and his face a deadly white. He almost knocked the woman over as he rushed down the stairs and disappeared out the door.

Mrs. Hall heard the stranger laughing wildly as he slammed the bedroom door shut.

Meanwhile, Dr. Cuss had fled to the home of Reverend Bunting. He burst into the churchman's study and gasped, "I think I've lost my mind! Do I look insane?"

The startled reverend looked up from the sermon he was writing and asked, "Insane? What are you raving about, Cuss?"

"It's that stranger at the inn," said the doctor breathlessly. "I've just had the most frightening experience with him. I went to call on him to get a donation to the Nurse Fund. When I opened the door to his room, he im-

His Face a Deadly White

mediately stuck his hands into his pockets and slumped down in his chair. All the while I was talking about the Nurse Fund, I kept staring at the bottles and powders and chemicals and test tubes everywhere. Then I asked him, point-blank, 'Are you working on a secret research project?'

"In between sneezes and sniffles from a nasty cold he's got, he snapped at me, 'If you must know, yes! I had searched for years and finally found the answer—the formula I needed for—. Never mind what for. All the ingredients were written on a piece of paper on my lab table when the breeze from an open window lifted the paper and carried it towards the fireplace. As it was being carried up the chimney, I rushed to reach out my arm to grab it, like this—'

"And he reached out his arm as if to show me how he had made a grab for the paper. But there was no hand—*just an empty sleeve!* My first thought was that he had an artificial arm

Just an Empty Sleeve!

and had taken it off. But then I began to wonder why, if he had no arm, what was keeping his sleeve up and open as he showed me how he reached.... No, there was nothing in that sleeve. I could look right into it, clear through to the elbow. He saw me staring and—"

"Yes, yes, go on."

"That's all. He never said a word, just glared at me as he put his sleeve back in his pocket and returned to his story of the paper that had blown up the chimney. But I wasn't about to let it go.

"'How can you move an empty sleeve?' I asked him.

"With that, he stood up and walked towards me until he was only inches away from my face. I don't mind telling you that having that bandaged face and those eerie glasses so close to my face sent shivers through my body.

"Then his voice came at me menacingly. 'Did you say it was an *empty* sleeve?'

"'Yes, I did.'

"His Face So Close to Mine"

"Then he slowly pulled his sleeve out of his pocket and raised it as if he was about to show it to me again. It was a strange feeling, seeing an empty sleeve coming at me like that. Then suddenly, something—it felt like a finger and a thumb—pinched my nose."

The reverend began to laugh.

"Don't laugh! There was nothing there!" shrieked Dr. Cuss in a panic. "I swear it!"

Reverend Bunting shook his head sadly as he looked at the doctor and wondered if the old gentleman was beginning to imagine things or perhaps had taken to drinking.

"Reverend, please believe me!" pleaded Dr. Cuss. "I even swung my arm at him and struck his sleeve. I felt like I was hitting an arm, but there wasn't any arm there! *I felt something, but I saw nothing! Nothing, I tell you! Nothing!* It was as if there was a ghost inside those clothes!"

The Reverend Began to Laugh.

"Someone's in the House!"

Chapter 4

A Puzzling Robbery

Some weeks later, near the end of May, a strange robbery occurred at the home of Reverend Bunting and his wife. Shortly before dawn one morning, Mrs. Bunting was awakened by the sound of bare feet tip-toeing softly outside her bedroom door and down the staircase.

"Wake up, Mr. Bunting," she whispered to her sleeping husband. "Someone's here in the house."

The reverend put on his glasses and slippers, then wrapped his wife's dressing gown around him. He armed himself with a poker from the fireplace and tip-toed out to the top of the staircase to listen. He heard noises coming from his study downstairs, followed by a loud, violent sneeze.

With Mrs. Bunting closely behind him, the reverend made his way down the dark stairs. The silence was broken only by the faint creaking of the stairs and some odd sniffles and rustling of papers in the study.

When they got to the bottom of the stairs, everything was quiet again. They stood at the half-open door and peered inside. The room that had been left in darkness the night before was now lit up by a candle on the desk. Its light revealed an open drawer, but there was no sign of a robber.

Suddenly, the silence was broken by the clinking of coins.

"He's found our housekeeping money," whispered Mrs. Bunting. "There's over two pounds in gold sovereigns in the drawer."

An Open Drawer

This news sent the reverend into action. Gripping the poker firmly, he rushed into the room, shouting fiercely, "Surrender! I've caught you!"

Reverend Bunting stopped so suddenly that his wife crashed into him.

"Why, the room's empty!" he cried, looking around him in astonishment.

"But I hear someone in here," insisted his wife. "I'm certain of it."

They stood gaping for a minute, then began to search the room. They probed under the desk, behind the curtains, outside the windows, up the chimney, and even in the wastepaper basket and coal scuttle.

"How can this be?" cried the bewildered reverend. "There's no one here, yet someone had to have lit the candle!"

"And the drawer!" cried Mrs. Bunting. "It's open and our money's gone!"

"A-CHOO!" came a violent sneeze from the hallway.

"Surrender! I've Caught You!"

The Buntings rushed out of the study, only to be stopped suddenly by the loud slamming of the kitchen door. As soon as they had caught their breath, they hurried towards the kitchen and flung open the door. Dawn was just beginning to break, and its faint light showed only an empty garden outside!

"The cellar!" cried the reverend. "Bring the candle and follow me."

A thorough search of the cellar and every cabinet and pantry in the kitchen revealed nothing. The Buntings then went on to inspect every room in the house.

By the time the candle had burned down in Mrs. Bunting's hand, the reverend and his wife were just as confused as when they had first seen it start to burn on the study desk.

"Bring the Candle and Follow Me!"

The Door was Slightly Open.

Chapter 5

Unwinding the Bandages!

At six o'clock on the same morning of the mysterious robbery at the Buntings, Mr. and Mrs. Hall discovered that the bolts on the front door of the inn had been slid back and that the door was slightly open.

"I locked the door last night before we went to bed," said Mrs. Hall. "Who could—"

"Who else?" said her husband, pointing up to the stranger's room. "Let's go check."

As they hurried up the stairs, Mr. Hall heard a cough coming from somewhere and thought it was from his wife in front of him.

Mrs. Hall heard the same cough and believed it was from her husband behind her.

At the top of the stairs, they knocked at the door, but got no reply.

"Try the door," said Mrs. Hall.

Mr. Hall turned the knob, and the door opened easily.

"There's no one in the bed and no one in the room either," he whispered to his wife.

But Mrs. Hall was staring in amazement at the big armchair near the fireplace. "Look!" she gasped. "There's his coat and trousers and shoes and eyeglasses on the chair! And his hat's hanging on top of the bed post."

"And there, on the table, all his bandages are piled up in a heap!" added her husband. "His clothes are here, but he's not!"

"This is all a very curious business," said Mrs. Hall, going over to the bed. She put her hand on the pillow, then under the covers and announced, "They're all cold, so he's been out of bed for an hour or more."

All His Bandages Piled in a Heap!

Just then, a most extraordinary thing happened. The blankets and sheets gathered themselves together, leaped up into a peak, then jumped over the foot of the bed onto the floor! It was followed by the stranger's hat hopping off the bed post and whirling through the air into Mrs. Hall's face!

The next moment, they heard a bitter laugh in front of them. The armchair turned itself on its side and flung the stranger's coat, trousers, shoes, and glasses to the floor. The chair seemed to be propelling its four legs through the air, charging at Mrs. Hall.

The innkeeper screamed and whirled around to her husband behind her. The chair slowed slightly and came to rest against her back. Then it pushed the two out of the room.

The door slammed violently, and the lock snapped shut. Then everything was still.

Mrs. Hall fell against her husband, almost in a faint. "It's evil spirits, I swear!"

"Now calm down, Jenny," he said. "There's

The Chair Charged at Mrs. Hall!

got to be an explanation. Come downstairs."

Once Mrs. Hall had a cup of tea to steady her nerves, she told her husband, "George, we've got to lock him out. He's put evil spirits into the furniture in his room."

"What about my room?" boomed a muffled voice coming down the staircase. It was the bandaged stranger glaring angrily at them from behind his large blue glasses. "You have no business in my room! Stay out and leave me alone!" With that, he stormed back up the stairs and slammed his door shut.

"W-we were just up in his room and he wasn't there," gasped Mrs. Hall. "How could he come down—?"

Her puzzled husband just shook his head. And for the next six hours, no one went near the stranger's room. Mrs. Hall even refused to answer his bell when the man rang it. "I suppose he wants food," she told her husband angrily. "But he can go to the devil!"

By noon, the usual customers had gathered

"No Business in My Room!"

at the bar. Everyone was talking about the mysterious robbery at Reverend Bunting's house. The conversation came to a sudden halt when the stranger, in his hat, gloves, and long coat, walked into the bar.

He glared at Mrs. Hall and demanded, "Why didn't you serve me my breakfast? And why haven't you answered my bell?"

"Why haven't you paid your bill?" she snapped back. "It's been five days since I gave it to you."

"I told you I didn't have the money then, but was expecting it in the mail any day," he replied angrily.

"Well, no money, no food, no roo—"

The stranger seemed to realize he was at the woman's mercy, and his voice softened as he added politely, "But I *do* have it now."

"Oh? And where'd you suddenly get it?" she demanded, remembering the talk at the bar about the Bunting robbery that morning. "And you've also got some explaining to do about my

The Stranger Walked Into the Bar.

furniture. What did you do to my chair upstairs? And how'd you get into your room when we found it empty at six o'clock this morning? Guests of my inn come and go by the doors, and you *didn't*!"

Suddenly the stranger raised his gloved hands and stamped his foot. "STOP!" he shouted angrily.

Mrs. Hall backed away and became silent.

"You don't understand who I am or what I am," he said with an eerie calmness. "But by Heaven, I'll show you!"

He put his hand in front of his face, then withdrew it. The center of his face where his nose had been was nothing but a black hole. "Here," he said, placing something soft and rubbery in Mrs. Hall's hand.

The woman looked down at her open palm. When she saw what that *something* was, she staggered back against the bar and dropped it to the floor, shrieking, "It's his nose! He's taken off his nose!"

"It's His Nose!"

The stranger ignored her and the gasps and cries from the villagers at the bar. His gloved hand then removed his hat and pulled off his eyeglasses. With a violent gesture, he tore off his long whiskers and patches of hair, then began unwinding the bandages from his head.

The horrified villagers backed away in terror. They could hardly believe what they were seeing. They were prepared to see some scars, to see a disfigured face, to see some kind of atrocity. But no one was prepared to see *nothing!*

Mrs. Hall screamed hysterically as she darted away from the bar and flew towards the door. Everyone in the room followed, tumbling over each other in panic.

The only man who remained inside the Coach and Horses was a figure dressed in trousers, gloves, and a coat with a turned-up collar. But above that collar was nothing, nothing at all!

Unwinding the Bandages

A Crowd Running Away

Chapter 6

Escape from an Angry Mob

The villagers in Iping heard shouts and shrieks coming from the crowd that was running away from the Coach and Horses. But the curious villagers began running *towards* the inn, eager to learn what the excitement was all about.

Once Mrs. Hall was a safe distance away, she collapsed in her husband's arms, as the crowd tried to explain the eerie happenings.

"It was a man without a head!"

"It was some magician's trick!"

"It was an evil spirit sent by the devil!"

"Hold up there!" called a voice from the rear of the crowd. It was Mr. Jaffers, the village constable.

"He's inside, the man without a head," called Mr. Hall.

"Well, head or no head, Hall, I'm here to arrest him."

Hall led the constable inside and up to the stranger's room. "Do your duty, constable," he said, flinging open the door.

Jaffers marched in, with Hall following.

"That's him," said Hall, pointing to a headless figure holding a piece of bread and a chunk of cheese in his gloved hands.

From the emptiness above the collar of the figure came an angry demand. "What's the meaning of this?"

"I'm here to do my duty and arrest you, head or no head," said Jaffers.

"Stay away from me," warned the Invisible Man, backing away from the constable.

Suddenly, the food dropped. Off came the

"I'm Here to Arrest You, Head or No Head!"

stranger's left glove, and Jaffers found it slapping him in the face. The constable managed to grip the man by his handless left wrist and clutched his invisible throat.

Despite a hard kick on his leg, the constable held on. The two men clutched and hit each other until both crashed to the ground.

"Grab his feet!" shouted Jaffers.

But before Hall could help, a hard kick in the ribs sent him flying against his wife's favorite cabinet.

Jaffers managed to pin the headless man down, then get on top of him. But he soon found himself rolled over on his back.

The stranger stood up over the constable and quietly said, "I surrender." Then he pulled off his right glove.

Two invisible hands then quickly opened the buttons along the front of his jacket. The jacket and trousers stooped over and began fumbling with his shoes and socks.

Standing above the stooped-over stranger,

Pinning the Headless Man

Hall exclaimed, "He's not a man at all! Look inside his collar and into his clothes. It's all emptiness inside." He tried to push his hand into the open blackness, only to pull it back suddenly with a cry of pain.

"I wish you'd keep your fingers out of my eyes," came a voice from somewhere above the clothes. "I'm all here, head, hands, legs, and all the rest. It happens that I'm invisible, but that doesn't give anyone the right to poke me to bits or to arrest me!"

By now, several other villagers had come into the room, and they heard the constable announce, "I'm arresting you on charges of breaking into a house and stealing money. And I need to handcuff you too."

"Nonsense!" cried the Invisible Man. "I'll come along to prove my innocence, but I will not allow handcuffs!"

"But I have my orders and it's the proper procedure," protested the constable.

The Invisible Man suddenly sat down and,

"He's Not a Man at All!"

before anyone realized what he was doing, he had kicked off his shoes and socks, then pulled off his trousers. The jacket began shaking itself loose from the shirt under it when Jaffers suddenly understood what the Invisible Man was doing.

"Here, stop that, I say!" he ordered as he reached out and pulled at the jacket, only to have it slide off in his hands. "Hold him!" he cried to the others. "If he gets his shirt off too, we'll never find him."

But a moment later, a fluttering white shirt was rushing around the room. It swung around in front of Hall and planted a hard blow in the man's face. Then it lifted itself up as if it were being pulled over a man's head. Jaffers made a grab for it, but succeeded only in helping to pull it off. In return, he was smashed in the mouth by an invisible fist.

By now, every arm in the room was striking out, hitting at the air or at each others' faces or heads. Cries of "Hold him!" and "Don't let

A Fluttering White Shirt

him get away!" filled the room. The furious swinging and hitting continued, causing bloody noses, black eyes, broken teeth, and smashed jaws.

Suddenly Jaffers yelled, "I've got something!"

The struggling crowd shot out into the hallway as Jaffers pushed his way through, holding tightly to his invisible prisoner. Then a hard kick forced his knees to crumple under him, and he loosened his hold on the Invisible Man. He felt himself being pushed down the steps and hitting his head on the hard stone floor, where he lay, unconscious and bleeding.

A woman standing in the inn doorway felt something push her aside. A dog in the road yelped as something kicked it. And an old man on a bicycle was thrown off into a ditch by an unseen force.

The Invisible Man had made his escape!

Making His Escape!

Mr. Thomas Marvel

Chapter 7

Mr. Thomas Marvel

About a mile and a half out of Iping, a tramp sat with his bare feet in a ditch at the side of the road. In front of him were two pairs of boots, both charity gifts. Mr. Thomas Marvel was trying to decide which pair to put on. One was four sizes too large, and the other had soles too thin for damp weather.

Marvel's furry silk top hat tilted onto his wrinkled, leathery face as he looked up, wondering whether the day would stay dry or whether a spring rain would fall before evening. He had loosened his coat around his short, stout body when he sat down in the ditch hours ago, and now, as he studied his boots, he began to retie the twine that held his coat together in places where buttons once did that job.

From behind Thomas Marvel came a voice that interrupted his concentration. "They're both rather ugly."

"That's true," agreed the tramp without bothering to turn around. "But I can't decide which is uglier. What kind are ye wearin'?" And he turned his head over his shoulder to inspect the speaker's boots.

But where boots should have stood, he saw neither legs nor boots. So he turned his head over his other shoulder, but found no boots or legs there either.

"Where are ye hidin'?" he asked, getting down on all fours and crawling in a circle to look. But he still found nothing.

"Am I drunk? Was I talkin' to myself?" he wondered, scratching his long, bushy beard.

"Where Are Ye Hidin'?"

"Don't be alarmed," came the voice again. "You're not drunk."

"Are ye some kind of ventriloquist? Or are ye buried somewhere in the ground?"

"I'm neither a ventriloquist nor buried in the ground, my good man."

Marvel stood up and turned himself around slowly several times. "I could swear I heard a voice talkin' to me."

"Of course you did."

Marvel suddenly felt himself grabbed by the collar and shaken violently.

"It's worryin' about those fool boots that's made my mind go daft. Or maybe it's ghosts."

"It's neither one."

"Then it's my imagination playin' tricks."

"We'll see if it's your imagination when I throw some stones at you." And from several feet away came a stream of small pebbles. Some grazed Marvel's shoulder, while others bounced off his bare feet into the ditch.

"Am I still your imagination?"

A Stream of Small Pebbles

Marvel sat down in a daze. "How can stones fling themselves? How can stones talk?"

"It's very simple. It's not the stones, it's me—an invisible man."

"Of course, anyone could see that. Ha! Why don't ye tell me where yer hidin'?"

"I'm not hiding. I'm invisible, and I'm here, just a few feet in front of you."

"Aw, come on. I'm not blind. I may be a tramp, but I'm not ignorant. Ye can't be just thin air."

"But I am. You can look through me because I'm invisible. I'm really a human being who needs food and drink and some clothing to cover myself."

"If yer a human bein', let me take yer hand and—*Lord!* Ye made me jump, grippin' my hand so tight!"

Marvel touched the hand that had closed around his wrist. Then his fingers traveled up the invisible muscular arm, crossed an invisible throbbing chest, and stroked an invisible

86

An Invisible Muscular Arm

bearded face.

"Lord! This is amazin'!" he cried. "Why, I can see clear through ye to spot that rabbit runnin' across the field." Then he looked at the invisible stomach even more closely and asked hesitantly, "Have ye eaten bread and cheese a while ago?"

"Yes, and they haven't been thoroughly digested into my system yet, so you can still see them."

"Amazin'! How do ye manage this invisible trick?"

"It's a long story, and I'll tell you about it another time. For now, I need help. I've been wandering through the countryside, naked and helpless. I've been in such a rage that I've been ready to commit murder! Then I came upon you and said to myself, 'Here's an outcast that society has rejected, just like it has rejected me. Perhaps he'd like to travel with me and help me.'"

"And how could *I* help you, Mr. Invisible?"

"Have Ye Eaten Bread and Cheese?"

"First with clothes and shelter, then later, with other things. Will you?"

Marvel backed away from the voice. "Look here, I'm just an ignorant tramp," he pleaded. "I can't be of any help to ye. Just let me go. Let me be on my way."

"No! You *must* help me. I've chosen you out of all those people back in Iping. Not only can you help me, but I can do great things for you. Just imagine what power an invisible man has!"

The voice paused, then sneezed loudly before it went on menacingly. "But if you betray me . . . if you don't follow my orders—"

Marvel felt a light tap on his shoulder, and he jumped back in terror at the touch. "I w-won't b-betray ye," he stammered, backing away still farther. "Don't ever think that. All Thomas Marvel will ever want to do is help ye, Mr. Invisible Man. I swear it!"

"I W-won't Betray Ye!"

Out of Breath and Upset

Chapter 8

A Man Enraged!

By midday, Iping had returned to normal. The people who believed in the Invisible Man breathed a sigh of relief that he had gone away, and those who doubted that he existed chose to make jokes about the incident at the Coach and Horses Inn that morning.

It was about four o'clock in the afternoon that a short, stout tramp was seen entering the village. He seemed out of breath and upset, and appeared to be talking to himself as he headed towards the Coach and Horses.

Mr. Thomas Marvel ignored the people at

the bar and climbed the stairs leading to the Invisible Man's room. He opened the door to find Dr. Cuss and Reverend Bunting seated at a table examining three big notebooks, each labeled "Diary."

"It's written in some kind of code," the doctor was saying.

"Either that or some strange lang—"

"I say there," said a voice at the door.

Both men looked up in panic, half-fearing that the voice belonged to the Invisible Man. But seeing only a rosy-faced tramp, they both smiled with relief.

"If you're looking for the bar, my good man, it's down below," said the doctor.

"Thank ye kindly," said Marvel as he backed out of the room and went downstairs. He stopped for a drink at the bar, then left the inn. Peering around to be sure no one was watching, Marvel hurried around to the side of the building below the Invisible Man's bedroom. He stood against the wall for a long while,

A Rosy-Faced Tramp

smoking his clay pipe, but his trembling hands and his repeated glances up to the window revealed how nervous he was.

Meanwhile, up in the bedroom, Dr. Cuss and Reverend Bunting still had their heads together, poring over the Invisible Man's notebooks. They were suddenly shocked to feel something cold and hard pushing at the backs of their necks. They tried lifting their heads, but the strong hands pressing on the metal fireplace poker forced their chins down onto the table and made them gasp for breath.

Then a voice whispered, "Don't move, you foolish men, or I'll brain you both!"

The reverend looked into the doctor's face, only inches from his own, and saw the same horror he himself was feeling.

"I'm sorry to handle you so roughly, but you've left me no choice," said the Invisible Man. "What gave you the right to search my room and pry into my private diaries?"

Before they could reply, their chins hit the

Gasping for Breath

table again, more violently than before. "And what have you done with my clothes?"

"W-we didn't see them. Mrs. Hall tidied up the room before we came in," said Dr. Cuss.

"I see. Well, then, since I need clothes, I'll just have to—" And the voice whispered something in the two men's ears.

"No!" cried the doctor. "I won't!"

"It's disgraceful!" shouted the reverend.

"You have no choice, gentlemen," said the Invisible Man as he let the men sit up. Then he walked to the window and opened it.

Across the road from the inn, Mr. Huxter, the tobacco shop owner, was sweeping his walk when he saw that window being opened. Minutes later, he saw three books tied together with a pair of suspenders and a big bundle wrapped in a blue tablecloth drop from that window into the outstretched arms of a tramp waiting below.

"Stop, thief! Stop!" cried Huxter as he ran into the road after the fleeing tramp.

"Stop, Thief! Stop!"

Huxter hadn't gone more than ten steps before his leg was grabbed in some mysterious way. The next moment, he found himself flying through the air, then smashing into the ground on his face, bloody and unconscious.

Huxter's cries of "Stop, thief!" had brought customers running out of the bar and into the road to join the chase. Only Mrs. Hall stayed behind, and that was to guard her cash register.

Suddenly, she heard the bedroom door open and saw Dr. Cuss running down the stairs and towards the front door. The old doctor was wearing only his underwear below his vest and jacket.

"Stop him! Grab him!" he cried. "He's got my trousers and every single stitch of the reverend's clothing."

Just behind him came Reverend Bunting, desperately trying to cover his body with the fireplace rug and the daily newspaper.

The two men didn't let their unusual ap-

Every Single Stitch!

pearance stop them from running out into the road and joining the crowd. Some tripped over Huxter's unconscious body. Others tumbled mysteriously and were flung to the ground and stepped on. These baffling attacks were enough to frighten the mob and persuade them to give up the chase and return to the safety of their homes.

The Invisible Man, however, followed them back to the village, destroying anything in his path. First, he chopped Mr. Hall's cart to splinters at the inn, then he threw a street lamp through the Buntings' parlor window and a wheelbarrow through Mr. Huxter's shop window. Next, he broke into Dr. Cuss's office and smashed every medicine bottle there. Finally, he cut all the telegraph wires from Iping to the outside world.

Once that rampage was over, the Invisible Man vanished from Iping. He was never heard from, seen or felt in the village ever again.

Smashing Every Medicine Bottle

Trudging Wearily Along

Chapter 9

An Unwilling Accomplice

By that evening, Thomas Marvel had left Iping far behind. He trudged wearily along the road, his arms loaded down with three books tied together and a bundle wrapped in a blue tablecloth. At every turn in the road, he peered eagerly around him, hoping for a chance to escape.

But the Invisible Man seemed to sense what Marvel was thinking, and every so often invisible hands beat down on the tramp's shoulders and a voice warned, "If you try to escape from me, I swear I'll kill you!"

"I'm not trying to run away, I swear," protested Marvel tearfully. "I don't know these roads and I don't want to get lost."

"It's bad enough those fools in Iping know I'm invisible and my secret will soon be in the newspapers. Now, everyone everywhere will be looking for me. I must keep you with me to do what needs to be done."

"But I'm weak. I'm of no use to ye. I'd only ruin any plans ye might make."

"You'd better not!" warned the Voice. "Just follow my orders and you won't get hurt. I don't need that bundle of clothing in the table-cloth any longer, so toss it away by the side of the road. But you'd better guard my books with your life!"

They walked most of the night, stopping only for a few hours to rest under some trees.

The next morning, they arrived at the small seaside town of Port Stowe, where they waited for the bank to open. Then, while the streets were still fairly empty, Marvel stood

Waiting for the Bank to Open

outside the bank and watched as money came flying through the air from inside the building and found its way into his coat and trousers pockets. Then he hurried away.

When he was safe distance from the bank, fear and exhaustion forced him to drop onto a bench outside a small inn. He laid the books on the bench beside him.

He hadn't been seated for long when an old seaman came out of the inn and sat down beside him. Although the seaman pretended to be reading his newspaper, his interest was roused by the books on the bench and by Marvel's bulging pockets.

"Amazing story in the newspaper," said the old seaman. "Seems there's an invisible man loose around these parts."

"No!" exclaimed Marvel. "Ye can't really believe in such things. *I* don't."

"Well, if the newspaper says it's happening, it must be true."

"What do they say he's been doin'?"

Stories in the Newspaper

"Everything! Says here he was discovered to be invisible when bandages were torn off his head during a fight and there was no head underneath them. Then the bloke tore off his clothes and got away 'cause no one could see him."

"That's astonishin'! And he just escaped, just like that? . . . Uh, did he have any pals helpin' him, does it say?"

"Doesn't say. But they think he took the road here to Port Stowe. Why, just think, man, if he was here and decided to rob you, you couldn't stop him 'cause you couldn't see him. And neither could the police."

All the while the seaman was talking, Marvel was glancing around him, listening for footsteps or any movements that would tell him where the Invisible Man was. But hearing nothing, he felt safe. Perhaps this was his chance to escape. So he bent his head towards the seaman and whispered, "Fact is, I know a thing or two about this Invisible Man. And

Listening for Footsteps

they're astonishin' things!"

"Indeed! Tell me!" cried the seaman.

"The fact is," began Marvel eagerly, "that I—OW!" With that, he gave a long, loud moan of pain and put his hand up to his left ear, which had just been smacked hard. Then, to explain away his mysterious "OW!" he quickly sobbed, "It's my tooth! It's achin' real bad! Got to be goin' now." And he picked up the books and hurried away from the bench.

"But the Invisible Man?" the seaman called after him.

"Not a word of it is true. I knew the chap who started that rumor, and he convinced the papers that it really happened."

"Why, you little potbellied old fool, letting me go on believing that you really knew something! Why, I've got a mind to—"

But by now, Marvel was being pulled along the road with rough jerks by an invisible hand on his shoulder and arm.

Pulled Along the Road

Dr. Arthur Kemp

Chapter 10

Shots in the Night

Later that day, in a house on the outskirts of the nearby town of Port Burdock, Dr. Arthur Kemp, a research scientist, was seated at a table in his top-floor study. The tall, thin young man with blond hair and moustache looked up from his microscope as the setting sun sent its last bright rays into the room.

Kemp put down his pen and stood up to stretch. He walked to the window, where a movement on the road caught his attention. It was a short, stout man frantically waving his arms as he ran, with some difficulty—it seemed to Kemp—towards town.

"Another fool!" muttered Dr. Kemp. "Running wildly and for no reason. Just like that idiot who ran into me this morning in town, shouting, 'The Invisible Man's coming, sir! You'd better hurry home!' I simply cannot understand how people can believe such foolish nonsense!"

But the people in Port Burdock who saw the terror on Thomas Marvel's perspiring face as he ran through town shouting warnings about the Invisible Man didn't think it was foolish nonsense. Not when they heard heavy breathing a few steps behind the tramp. Not when a dog playing in the road yelped from an invisible kick. Not when two boys huddled together were suddenly elbowed apart by an invisible arm. Not when a child was pulled from its mother and pushed to the side of the road by an invisible hand.

People screamed in terror as they ran to their homes. Panic spread through town along

People Screamed in Terror

with cries of "The Invisible Man is here!"

Those cries hadn't yet reached the inside of the Jolly Cricketer Inn when the door suddenly burst open and Thomas Marvel tumbled through it. His hat was gone and his coat was torn open at the neck, but he was still clutching the books in his arms. He threw his whole body against the door to slam it shut as he wept uncontrollably, "He's comin'! The Invisible Man's comin'! He's after me! For God's sake, help me!"

"Then the stories in the newspapers *are* true!" gasped the frightened barman.

"Quick, bolt the door!" ordered a policeman who had been having a drink at the bar.

"Lock me in!" begged Marvel. "I gave him the slip, but he's after me. He threatened to kill me and I know he will!"

Suddenly, a violent banging shook the bolted door from top to bottom.

"It's him!" shrieked Marvel as he looked around in a panic for a place to hide. "Don't let

"Lock Me In!"

him kill me!"

The barman pulled the tramp behind the bar as the banging was repeated.

"*Please* don't open the door!" screamed Marvel. "And be sure all the other doors to the inn are shut. He's as sly as the devil. If there's an unlocked door, he'll find it."

"Good Lord!" shrieked the barman. "There's the yard door and the back door and the kitchen—"

Just then, a door slammed. The barman rushed out of the bar towards the kitchen, but reappeared moments later carrying a large carving knife. "The kitchen door was closed, but the yard door was open. He may be in the house already."

The policeman took out his revolver just as the door from the bar to the kitchen burst open *by itself*! Marvel was suddenly pulled from behind the bar and flung across the room by an invisible force. The revolver cracked, and the large mirror behind the bar shattered and

The Revolver Cracked.

came smashing to the floor.

The barman and the policeman froze in their tracks and stared in wonder as invisible hands dragged Marvel, screaming, out of the bar and into the kitchen.

The policeman recovered his senses before the door could be bolted and rushed after them. He grabbed a wrist that was dragging Marvel, but a punch to his face sent him staggering back.

"I got him!" cried the barman, clawing at the air.

Finding himself suddenly freed by the attack, Marvel crawled between the legs of the fighting men. Then, the voice of the Invisible Man was heard shouting a cry of pain as the policeman stamped down hard on his foot. But he recovered immediately, and his unseen fists and legs flew out, sending the policeman doubled over to the ground.

In the confusion of the fighting, Marvel grabbed the books he had been guarding and

"I Got Him!"

crawled out of the bar, unseen. Once in the kitchen, he headed for the yard door.

Moments later, the bewildered men found themselves struggling with empty air.

"Where's he gone?" gasped the barman.

"Must have made his way out same as how he came in, through the yard door," said the policeman as he got to his feet. "Let's go."

No sooner had they entered the kitchen than a plate came whizzing by the policeman's head. "I'll show him!" he exclaimed as he raised his revolver and took aim at the open yard door.

Five shots rang out and sped into the night outside the door. Then all was silent.

"You must've hit him," said the barman. "I'll get a lantern and we'll see if we can feel around for his body."

A Plate Came Whizzing By.

The Sound of Gunshots

Chapter 11

Dr. Kemp's Visitor

While the fight was going on at the Jolly Cricketer, Dr. Kemp was completely absorbed in his research work, dividing his attention between his microscope and the notes he was making. All of a sudden, the sound of gunshots from Port Burdock sent him hurrying to the window.

"Looks like a crowd in front of the Cricketer," he muttered as he looked out towards the town. "I guess someone's had a bit too much to drink and is causing trouble."

With that, Kemp returned to his table and

to his work. For the next hour, his attention was once again on his work until the ringing of his doorbell interrupted him. He listened as his housekeeper went to answer it, but was surprised when she didn't knock at his study door to announce the visitor.

After several minutes, he went out into the hall and called down, "Who was at the door, Annie?"

"No one, sir. Must've been someone playing a trick, ringing and running off."

Even though Kemp returned to his work, he was restless for the next several hours.

Finally, at two o'clock in the morning, he put down his pen and picked up a candle to light his way down to his bedroom. Because he was a scientist with a scientist's curiosity, he stopped to examine a dark spot on the floor at the foot of the stairs at the bedroom level.

He bent down and touched the spot. "It's red and sticky, like drying blood. Oh, well, perhaps Annie had a slight accident. She'll probably

A Dark Spot

clean it up in the morning."

Putting the spot out of his mind, Kemp turned towards his bedroom. But when he spied the door open and the handle covered with blood, he gasped in astonishment.

"Good Lord!" he cried as he walked into the room. "There's a large blood stain on the bedspread and the sheet's all ripped. And my pillow's indented as if someone's been lying on it! What's happened in here?"

Just then, a voice in the room spoke. "Good Heavens! It's you, Kemp!"

Kemp looked around the room, but saw that he was the only person there. As a doctor and a scientist, he certainly didn't believe in voices from nowhere.

Then a sound near his washstand made him spin around abruptly. There, hanging in midair just before him, was a blood-stained bandage wrapped around something shaped like an arm. *But no arm was there!* Kemp was about to reach out to touch the bandage when

A Blood-Stained Bandage

a voice just inches away from him spoke.

"Don't be frightened, Kemp. You're not hearing things. I'm an invisible man."

Kemp stared at the bandage for several seconds, then stammered, "A t-talking bandage? . . . An in-invisible . . . m-man?"

"Yes, an invisible man."

"Then the talk in town this morning was true?" said Kemp, still not fully believing what he was hearing. "I thought it was nonsense when people said an invisible man was here. But why are you wearing a bandage?"

Kemp reached out to touch the bandage, but invisible fingers clamped down on his wrist and held it back. Frightened at the eerie touch, the doctor turned pale and tried to pull his hand away. But the grip on his wrist only tightened. Now desperate to free himself, Kemp beat at the air around him with wildly swinging arms.

But his invisible enemy was in control, and Kemp found himself being overpowered,

Wildly Swinging Arms

tripped and flung backwards onto his bed. When he tried to shout for help, a corner of the sheet was stuffed into his mouth and strong fingers tightened around his throat.

"Listen to reason, you fool!" cried the Invisible Man as Kemp fought wildly, kicking and punching him. "Stop this attack and lie still or I'll smash your face."

When Kemp finally stopped struggling, the voice explained, "I'm *really* an Invisible Man. It's no trick and no magic. I need your help. I don't want to hurt you, but if you behave like a stupid idiot, I'll have to. You know me, Kemp. We went to University College together. I'm Jack Griffin. Do you remember me?"

"Let me sit up and try to understand all this," said Kemp.

The Invisible Man backed off and let the young doctor sit up.

"Are you the Jack Griffin who won the college medal for chemistry?" Kemp asked.

"Yes. I'm that Griffin, only now I've made

Trying to Shout for Help

myself invisible."

"That's horrible! Why would you want to do such a devilish thing? And how did you—"

"Look, Kemp, I'm wounded and in pain, and tired and hungry. I'll explain later."

Kemp stared in astonishment as the blood-stained bandage moved across the room to a chair. The seat depressed a little as the Invisible Man sat in it.

"I'd like something to drink."

Kemp filled a glass with some whiskey and walked towards the chair. "Where shall I give it to you?" he asked.

The chair creaked, and Kemp felt the glass being pulled out of his hand. It came to a stop about twenty inches above the seat.

"You must be hypnotizing me," said Kemp.

"Nonsense!" said the voice as the glass tilted and the whiskey poured out of it, forming a small pool in midair. "Now, listen here! I'm starving, and freezing as well, since I've been running about with no clothes on. Do you have

"You Must Be Hypnotizing Me!"

a dressing gown?"

Kemp went to his closet and took out a long red robe. "Will this do?"

Invisible fingers took the robe from him. It fluttered weirdly in midair, straightened out upright, tied its belt, then sat down in the chair.

"Some underwear, socks, and slippers would help as well. And food."

"Of course, anything you need," said Kemp, going to his drawers to get the clothing the Invisible Man requested. "But this is the craziest thing I ever heard of in my life."

Still, Kemp went down to the kitchen and brought up some bread and meat. By now, the underwear, socks, and slippers were visible on the invisible body seated in the chair.

"Never mind knives and forks," said the voice, as a slice of cold meat was grabbed off the plate. It hung in midair as bites from invisible teeth gnawed away at it.

Kemp sat down on the edge of his bed, still

Bites From Invisible Teeth

shaking his head in disbelief. "Invisible!" he gasped. "Of all the strange—"

"Actually," interrupted the Invisible Man with a mouthful of food, "what's strange is that I should have had the good luck to accidentally stray into the house of someone I knew to get bandages for my wound. Even though my blood is invisible like the rest of me, it becomes visible as it clots, so you can see exactly where I was wounded."

"And how were you wounded?"

"There was a fool of a man—curse that Marvel!—who was supposed to be helping me. But he stole my money and my books instead."

"Did *he* shoot you?"

"No."

"Did *you* shoot him? Were those the shots I heard from town?"

"No, some fool at the inn fired at me.... But enough talk for now, Kemp. I'd like a cigar to finish off this meal."

Kemp brought him the cigar and sat back in

Bringing Him the Cigar

wonder as the smoke traveled through the Invisible Man's mouth, down his throat, and out his nostrils. "You must tell me how this was all done. How did you get like this?"

"Good Lord, man! Can't you see I'm totally exhausted and in pain from my wound?" the voice suddenly groaned, and the robe leaned forward with sleeves bent upward, supporting an invisible head on invisible hands. "Kemp, I've been on the run and haven't slept for three days and three nights."

"Well then, sleep now, here in my room."

"But if I sleep, Marvel will get away. Besides, I can't take the chance of being caught by the police."

Kemp sat forward, startled. "Police?"

The Invisible Man banged on the table with his fist. "Fool that I am!" he exclaimed. "I've put the idea into your head to turn me in, and now I can't even trust you!"

"Not at all!" protested Kemp. "I shall keep your secret. No one will know that you're here.

Down His Throat

I swear. You can lock yourself in this room, and you won't be disturbed."

"All right," said the Invisible Man with a yawn. "I *am* exhausted. I do accept your offer of this room, and I'm sorry that I can't explain everything to you tonight. But believe me when I assure you that becoming invisible *is* possible. I made that discovery some time ago and had hoped to keep it to myself. But now I see that I can't. I must have a partner. We can do such wonderful things together. But that's for tomorrow. For now, I must sleep or I shall die."

"Then good-night," said Kemp as he reached out and shook an invisible hand.

The robe followed him to the door and the voice uttered a final warning. "There had better not be any attempts to interfere with my plans or any attempts to capture me!"

Shaking an Invisible Hand

"Am I Dreaming?"

Chapter 12

A Wonderful Discovery?

As the door closed behind him and the key was turned in the lock, Dr. Kemp slapped his forehead with his hand. "Am I dreaming?" he asked himself in amazement. "Has the world gone mad...or have I?" Then he rubbed his bruised neck where invisible fingers had held him during the struggle. "No, it's not a dream. It's a fact, an undeniable fact!"

Kemp went downstairs into the small office where he sometimes saw patients, even though most of his practice of medicine was spent in research. After lighting the gas lamp, he gathered up the day's newspapers that his housekeeper had left there for him.

He began reading each one thoroughly, amazed at headlines like "Strange Story from Iping" and "Entire Village in Sussex Goes Mad." As he read, he learned of the strange happenings involving an invisible man who ran through the streets striking people, attacking a constable, humiliating a doctor and reverend, and terrorizing everyone.

When he had finished poring over every account, Kemp sat back, bewildered. "Why on earth was he chasing that tramp he called Marvel? There was no mention of an accomplice in any of these stories. He's not only invisible, but after reading these accounts, I'm convinced that he's mad as well! Mad enough to be capable of murder!"

Dr. Arthur Kemp spent the rest of the night pacing up and down in his office, trying to decide what to do. He was still in his office when his housekeeper knocked in the morning. He

Pacing Up and Down

gave her orders to serve breakfast for two upstairs in his study, but told her to stay downstairs on the ground floor of the house the entire day.

Kemp waited in his office until the morning papers came. They contained an account of the happenings at the Jolly Cricketer the night before. They also mentioned Thomas Marvel and quoted him as saying, "The Invisible Man made me stay with him for twenty-four hours." Marvel, however, did not bother to talk about the three books he had stolen from the Invisible Man or the man's money that now filled his pockets.

"I'm beginning to fear what that man might do," whispered Kemp. "He's a maniac, and he's here in my house, as free as air. What should I do? . . . Would I be breaking my word if I—?"

Kemp thought a while, then came to a decision. He went to his desk and wrote a brief note. He put it in an envelope and addressed it to "Colonel Adye, Port Burdock Police."

Coming to a Decision

Just as Kemp was handing the note to his housekeeper to deliver to town, a terrible noise came from his bedroom. Feet were rushing across the room, chairs were being flung and broken, and the washstand and glasses were being smashed on the floor.

Kemp whispered, "Hurry!" to the woman and ran upstairs.

The bedroom door was still locked from the night before, but was opened immediately at Kemp's loud knock.

"What's the matter?" he asked the headless robe. "What was all the smashing about?"

"Nothing," said the Voice above the robe. "Just a fit of temper. I forgot this arm was injured when I went to use it."

"You seem to have many of these outbursts of temper," said Kemp as he began picking up the broken glass and righting the overturned furniture.

When he had finished, he turned to the Invisible Man and said, "The papers are full of

"Hurry!"

news about you and the events in Iping and Port Burdock. Everyone is wondering where you are, but, of course, no one knows you're here or that I'm going to help you."

The Invisible Man began pacing and swearing under his breath. He didn't stop until Kemp suggested breakfast. At that, he followed the doctor upstairs to his study.

After a nervous glance out the window, Kemp sat down at the table opposite a headless, handless robe. He watched as invisible hands shook out the napkin and placed it in the lap of the robe.

"You must explain this invisibility of yours, Griffin," said Kemp. "Surely you must realize how curious I am at your wonderful discovery."

"Wonderful, yes, at the beginning. But now I'm not sure...not unless we can do great things with it. Listen as I tell you what I've been through."

A Headless, Handless Robe

"I Switched from Medicine to Physics."

Chapter 13

The Invisible Man's Story

"You probably didn't know that I switched my studies from medicine to physics when I was twenty-two. I was especially interested in the study of *light* and its relationship to solids and liquids, like the way a piece of glass becomes practically invisible in water when light passes through it."

"Yes, but man isn't transparent like glass is," said Kemp. "So what does this have to do with you?"

"Ah, but man *is* transparent. In fact, *he's more transparent!* Just think, Kemp, flesh,

157

bone, hair, nails, nerves—every part of man except the red of his blood and certain pigments, or coloring matter—are all made up of transparent, colorless tissue. I worked on these ideas for six years, never daring to tell a soul or publish my findings until I had everything perfected. All my research, every formula I developed, everything I've done is written in code in those three notebooks Thomas Marvel stole from me. That's why I must hunt him down and get them back."

"But the blood and the pigments—how did you make *them* invisible?"

"That took another three years. I almost had to give up my research because of money, but I was so determined to go on with my work, I stole the money from my father. But the money wasn't his and he shot himself." With a deep sigh, the Invisible Man got up from the table and went to the window. Kemp stared silently for a few moments at the back of the headless figure. Then a sudden thought made

"I Stole Money From My Father!"

him get up and go to the window. He took the arm of the dressing gown and led the Invisible Man back to his chair.

"You're tired, Griffin. I don't think you should be up and around yet. Please sit down and go on with your story."

Kemp placed himself between the Invisible Man's chair and the window, blocking out any view of the road to town.

The voice went on. "I was able to buy all the equipment I needed with the stolen money and continue my experiments. At first, I made a piece of white wool fabric invisible. What a strange feeling it was to put my hand into empty air and feel the fabric as solid as ever. I even threw it on the floor, then had trouble finding where it was."

"Amazing!" cried Kemp.

"The next part of the experiment was even more amazing. A starving neighborhood cat strayed into my lab, and I suddenly realized that here was my next experiment."

A Starving Cat

"And did you make the cat invisible?"

"Almost. I mixed the drugs I had developed with some food and laid her down on a pillow. She was unconscious for several hours while every part of her slowly became invisible. Only the green pigment at the back of her eyes remained visible when she awoke. The last I saw of her were two shiny green circles jumping out an open window.

"But the success of this experiment set my brain on fire, and I began to dream about all the wonderful things an invisible man could do in this world. I also knew that my money was almost gone and I owed my landlord back rent. The thought of making myself invisible and disappearing suddenly became irresistible, so I began to make plans.

"That very day, I made a package of my three notebooks and mailed it to myself at a package pick-up office on the other side of London. Then I returned to my room, mixed the drugs, and drank the potion.

"Every Part of Her Became Slowly Invisible!"

"As I sat waiting for it to work, a knock at the door woke me from my sick, drowsy state. I opened the door to find my landlord about to thrust an eviction notice into my hands. As he lifted his eyes to my face, he let out a cry, dropped the paper, and ran down the hall, shrieking. I shut the door and hurried to my mirror. When I saw what I looked like, I understood his terror. My face had turned as white as stone!

"The horrible suffering that followed that night can't be described. My body felt as if it were on fire. I was sick to my stomach. I fainted often, then regained consciousness. I sobbed and groaned and talked to myself. I wanted to die, but I also wanted to live.

"By morning, the pain had passed. I lay in my bed looking down at my hands, which now had the look of clouded glass. As the day wore on, they became clearer and thinner until I could place them in front of my eyes and see the room through them. Next came my arms

"My Body Felt as if it Were on Fire!"

and legs, then my bones and blood.

"By the end of the day, I struggled to get up. I felt like a baby just learning to walk, for I was stepping on legs I couldn't see. I stumbled to my mirror and saw nothing in its reflection except the room behind me.

"Just then, a loud banging came at my door, and the angry voice of my landlord demanded that I open it or he and his sons would break it down. When I didn't reply, they began attacking the door with axes.

"I was desperate! I didn't want them to see the chemicals and the equipment I had been using for my experiments, so I piled up a heap of paper and rubbish and turned on the gas. As I headed for the open window, I tossed a match onto the pile and waved good-bye to everything I owned."

"You mean you burned the entire house down and risked other lives?"

"Down to the ground!" sneered the Invisible Man. "It was the only way to be sure no one

"I Tossed a Match onto the Pile."

discovered my secret. As I watched the blaze from the end of the street, I thought of the wild and wonderful things I could now do without getting caught!"

"Where did you go then?"

"I headed for the package pick-up office to retrieve my books. How I enjoyed myself on the way, slapping men on the back as I passed or flinging their hats off their heads or dumping packages out of women's arms or swinging baby carriages around in circles! How amusing it was to see everyone's startled expressions!

"But I soon found myself being bumped into by deliverymen, kicked by passing horses, and nearly crushed by afternoon crowds on the street. Dogs who couldn't see me, but who have an extraordinary sense of smell, began sniffing around me and following me. In addition, my bare feet were becoming sore from the rough stones and frozen mud on the road, and my naked body was beginning to tremble from

"Dogs Began Sniffing Around Me!"

the cold of the January day. It had never occurred to me that invisible or not, I was still affected by the weather.

"I also found small boys a problem. As I hurried along the street, two of them stood pointing down at the mud in curiosity.

" 'Look!' said one. 'There's footprints runnin' along, but no one's makin' 'em.'

" 'And see, there's some blood in one o' the prints,' added the other.

"I began to run, but the two boys followed, shouting, "Feet! Running feet!"

"Soon a crowd was trailing after them. I managed to stay ahead of them all for several blocks until I was able to find a dry stretch of road. I stopped then, dried my muddy feet, and continued on with no tracks for my pursuers to follow."

At the mention of *pursuers*, Dr. Kemp glanced nervously out the window, at the same time urging the Invisible Man, "Go on, Griffin. What then?"

"Feet! Running Feet!"

Outside the Omnium Department Store

Chapter 14

A Wild Threat

The Invisible Man went on. "The sky that day threatened more snow before nightfall. If the flakes settled on me, they'd expose me. I had to find someplace warm, where I could rest and think and make plans.

"I had no way of getting inside locked houses and I couldn't risk opening inn doors to let an invisible body enter. But when I found myself standing outside the Omnium department store, I knew I could get inside to find the food, clothing, and money I needed.

"I waited until the doorman opened the door

for a customer and hurried in with her. I wandered about the store until I found a warm corner beside a pile of mattresses. I sat there for several hours, making my plans. Once the store closed, I would find something to eat, gather the clothing I'd need for my disguise, take some money from the store's registers, get a good night's sleep on one of the store's beds, then go out the next day and pick up my notebooks."

"Did it work?"

"Not as I had hoped. I managed to locate all the money, clothing, and food I'd need, then went to sleep on a pile of soft quilts stacked in the middle of the floor.

"But the store opened before I was awake, and I was sighted. I jumped up and began to run wildly past shocked salespeople. Up one aisle and down another I darted, a headless figure in trousers, coat, gloves, shoes, and hat, until I realized I had to get them all off if I was to escape. So, I dropped behind a counter and

A Headless Figure

pulled off everything.

"And did they find you?" asked Kemp.

"Certainly not. I managed to get out as the police were coming in. But now I had no clothing, no money . . . and no idea what to do next. And I couldn't eat while I was on the run, for the food would be visible inside me until my stomach fully digested it."

"I never thought of that," said Kemp. "But was the snow a problem?"

"No, it had already melted. But it did alert me to other dangers of weather. Rain would make me a watery outline, much like the outline of a bubble, and fog would do the same. So, even though snow wasn't a problem, the day was very cold and windy and I knew I had to find clothing fast. I was already beginning to feel a cold coming on and had to stifle my sneezes as I hurried through the streets.

"A while later, I had better luck in a small costume shop on a deserted side street, where no one saw me open a door. The owner was in

"Rain Would Make a Watery Outline."

the back eating his lunch, but he must have had very sharp ears, for he hurried out to the front when I entered and looked around. Seeing nothing suspicious, he returned to the kitchen to his meal, or so I thought.

"I was standing in front of a rack of clothes when I saw the man return, this time waving a revolver and shouting, 'Who's there? I heard you. You'd better come out or else.' And he let go several shots, one of which missed me only by inches. . . . But I took care of him!"

"Good Heavens, man! Did you kill him?"

"No, at least I don't think so. I hit him from behind with a stool and gagged him and tied him up in a sheet so he wouldn't see me putting on my disguise. . . . Oh, Kemp, don't glare at me like I was a murderer. It had to be done. He had a revolver and I couldn't let him describe me—"

"But the man was in his own house and you were robbing him!"

"So, you're blaming me for that, are you?

"I Hit Him from Behind with a Stool!"

And what exactly are you planning to do?"

Kemp drew in his breath and suddenly changed his tone. He couldn't risk angering Griffin at that moment. "Yes, I guess you're right. You were in a fix and had to defend yourself. So what did you do next?"

"I gathered the clothing I needed, along with dark glasses, whiskers, a wig, and of course all the silver shillings and gold sovereigns the man had in his cash drawer. I was now ready to go out into the world!"

"And you left the man tied up in the sheet?" asked Kemp, as he paced back and forth in front of the window.

"Why not? He probably untied himself or kicked his way out eventually. My only concern at that moment was to find food. I knew I couldn't go into a restaurant and eat in public, so I chose one that had private dining rooms, explaining that I was badly disfigured and preferred to eat alone."

The Invisible Man paused and seemed to

Ready to Go Out

turn his body towards Kemp, who was still pacing in front of the window.

Eager to keep his guest talking, the doctor asked, "And you went to Iping next?"

"Yes. I shipped my books there ahead of me, along with the clothing and equipment I had bought. I planned to work in Iping, undisturbed. I had one hope—and I still have it— that I can get back to being visible . . . but *only when I choose* and only after I've done all that I intend to do invisibly. And that, Kemp, is what I need your help for."

"I won't help you attack people like those you attacked in Iping."

"They'll recover. But that Thomas Marvel will not, not when I get my hands on him! He'll pay for what he's done! And so will anyone else who tries to interfere with my plans! I'll kill them! I'll kill them all!"

"I'll Kill Them All!"

Spotting Three Men

Chapter 15

"Traitor!"

After spotting three men coming up the road towards his house, Dr. Kemp forced himself to walk away from the window. He positioned himself between the Invisible Man and the window, and calmly asked, "What were you planning to do in Port Burdock?"

"I had considered taking a ship south to Spain. There, I could go without clothes in the hot weather and people wouldn't be looking for a man wrapped up in bandages."

"That sounds reasonable."

"Those *were* my plans before I had the good

fortune of blundering into your house. Now, everything's changed. You, Kemp, are a man who can understand what I want to do. You can understand the possibilities that are ahead of us. You are much better equipped to help me than that filthy brute who robbed me! You can provide me with a hiding place where I can sleep and eat and rest. With all that, I can break into houses, rob anything we want, even kill anyone...and escape! And it *is* killing we must do, Kemp! And my first victim will be that thieving tramp!"

"Y-you ought to g-get your books from him f-first," Kemp stammered nervously, trying to speak over the sound of the footsteps he thought he heard outside. "The newspapers say he's in the police station, locked up at his own request in their strongest cell."

"That won't stop me! Nothing will stop me! Ha! Ha! Ha!"

The maddened laughter covered the sound of the front door opening as Griffin continued

The Front Door Opened.

his wild ranting and raving.

"We will kill wisely, Kemp. We will establish a Reign of Terror. We will capture your town of Burdock and terrorize it. And all who disobey us we will kill! Kill, I say! Kill! Kill!"

"But, Griffin, why put me in such a position?" Kemp said, trying to keep his voice calm. "After all, I—"

"*Hush!* What's that noise downstairs?"

"I didn't hear anything," said Kemp, trying to distract him. "Now listen, Griffin, I simply can't agree with your plan. It would be better for the world if you'd publish your experiments. Let everyone know of your discovery. Perhaps there's a scientist out there who can help—"

The Invisible Man interrupted the doctor. "I hear footsteps coming up the stairs. If you've told anyone I'm here—"

"No, not a soul!"

"You'd better not have!" cried the Invisible Man as he started towards the door.

Footsteps on the Stairs!

Kemp jumped between him and the door before the Invisible Man could reach it.

"Traitor!" shrieked the voice. "You *have* betrayed me!"

The dressing gown suddenly opened, and the Invisible Man began to remove his clothes.

Kemp sprang to the door and flung it open. Immediately behind him came a flying dressing gown, still on an invisible body.

Kemp pushed the Invisible Man back into the room and slammed the door behind him. One turn of the key, and he would have his prisoner safely locked inside. But the slamming of the door jiggled the key. It fell out of the lock and dropped to the floor.

Kemp's face went white. He tried to grip the door handle with both hands. But it was jerked open, and an invisible body wedged itself between the door and the frame.

Invisible fingers reached out and gripped Kemp's throat, forcing him to let go of the handle to defend himself. Then the dressing gown

Slamming the Door!

was out in the hall, and Kemp felt himself being pushed back into a corner at the top of the stairs. The next moment, an empty dressing gown was on top of him.

Halfway up the stairs, Colonel Adye, the Chief of Police, was staring in shock at the sight of Dr. Kemp beneath a wildly tossing dressing gown. The next moment, that same dressing gown was hurling itself at him. Invisible fingers gripped at his throat. Invisible knees rammed into his belly. Then this invisible nothingness hurled him headlong down the stairs.

Two startled policemen who had been a few steps behind Colonel Adye hurried to their chief's aid as the front door slammed shut with a bang.

"He's gone!" cried Kemp, staggering down the stairs, his clothes torn and his face bloody. He held up a limp dressing gown as he gasped, "It's too late! We've lost him!"

Shock!

"He's Mad!"

Chapter 16

The Hunt for the Invisible Man

Dr. Kemp was too distraught to speak for several minutes after the door had slammed. Finally, he led Colonel Adye into his office and poured them both a drink.

"He's mad!" gasped Kemp. "He's no longer human. He's selfish and concerned only with his own evil schemes. He has wounded men and doesn't care. He'll kill as well, unless we can stop him."

"We *must* catch him," said Adye.

"And we must do it before he leaves this district. Once he gets away, he'll roam the countryside killing anyone who gets in his way. He plans a reign of terror, starting here in Port Burdock. You must use police at train stations, on the roads, and at the ports. You must call out the army for help. The only thing that might keep him here for a short while is his determination to get his notebooks from Marvel."

"Yes, yes, the chap in our jail."

"Also, Colonel, you must prevent that madman from sleeping and eating. Houses, inns, and shops must be kept locked so he can't find a place to rest or food to eat. We must pray for cold nights and rain. He can't risk being outdoors where his outline would show. He'll be forced to seek shelter, and then we can trap him. I tell you, Adye, if we don't, I'm afraid to think what will happen to us all!"

"Since you know so much about him, Kemp, I think it would be helpful if you came to town to help us organize the search."

Kemp agreed, and the two men set off for

"Prevent His Sleeping and Eating!"

the police station in Kemp's carriage. On the way, the doctor suggested, "Get dogs. Even though they can't see him, they can pick up his scent."

"Good idea! I know a chap who raises and trains bloodhounds. Anything else?"

"Remember that his food shows inside him until it's digested, so he has to hide after he eats. Also, send your men into every clump of shrubs to search and make sure that they keep their weapons hidden. He can't carry any around with him for long, but he *can* use any that he snatches up."

"Good! Anything else?"

"Yes. Spread powdered glass on the roads so his feet will get cut. It's cruel, I know, but not as cruel as what this madman might do to others. He's no longer human, and our only chance is to keep ahead of him and outsmart him."

By two o'clock on that hot June afternoon, word had spread throughout the countryside

"Get Dogs!"

that the Invisible Man was a dangerous criminal and had to be wounded, captured, or, if necessary, killed! Mounted police rode from cottage to cottage warning people to lock their doors and stay inside. All schools were closed and children taken home. Warnings were posted on every lamp post in nearby towns, and telegraph messages went out to police throughout England. Every passenger train traveled with locked doors; all freight trains were canceled. In an area twenty miles around Port Burdock, men armed with guns, clubs, and bloodhounds roamed the countryside, hoping to pick up the scent.

One man, however, became the innocent victim of the Invisible Man's madness. He was Lionel Wicksteed, a middle-aged caretaker on his way home from work for lunch. Why he was attacked, no one knows, but Wicksteed was a peace-loving man who would never provoke violence from anyone. He had been beaten around his head with an iron bar, broken

An Innocent Victim

off from a fence, the police figured. The bloody bar had been left beside the man's body.

Police considered the possibility that the Invisible Man may have been carrying the bar to defend himself, without actually planning to use it to murder anyone. They also thought that Wicksteed may have come upon the iron bar moving strangely through the air along the road and had followed it, simply out of curiosity, perhaps even striking at it with his walking stick.

Soon after the discovery of Wicksteed's body, reports of the Invisible Man came from people throughout the area. Some men working on a farm in Hintondean, a town several miles inland from Port Burdock, heard a strange voice wailing and laughing, sobbing and groaning as it crossed a field and echoed into the hills beyond.

When Colonel Adye learned of this, he told Kemp, "The Invisible Man probably realized that you gave us the information he had con-

A Strange Voice Wailing and Laughing

fided to you and that we're now using it to try to trap him. He has most certainly discovered that houses and inns are locked, that guards are at railway stations, that proclamations are on every lamp post in every town, and that soldiers and dogs are combing the fields for him."

"But he's clever," said Kemp. "And by now, he's also desperate!"

Yet, in spite of all those precautions, the Invisible Man somehow managed to avoid capture. The police believed he even managed to eat and sleep during the twenty-four hours following his escape.

Not only that, but the Invisible Man awoke that morning with new energy, feeling more powerful, more embittered, and full of more hatred than ever. Added to this was a horrible desire for revenge! He was ready for his last great struggle against the world—a struggle he was determined to win!

Proclamations on Every Lamp Post

PEDPLE OF PORT BURDOCK:
You have been amazingly
clever, though I cannot
imagine what you have
to gain by your cleverness.
You have proven that you
ar...

A Strange Letter

Chapter 17

The Siege of Dr. Kemp's House

The afternoon mail to Dr. Kemp's house brought an envelope postmarked that morning in Hintondean. The doctor was at lunch when his housekeeper brought it to him. He opened it and found a strange letter written in pencil on a greasy sheet of paper. He read:

"*People of Port Burdock:*

You have been amazingly clever, though I cannot imagine what you have to gain by your cleverness. You have proven that you are against me by chasing me all night and trying to keep me from eating and sleeping. But I have succeeded in doing both.

The Terror is about to begin and today is the first day. Tell your Colonel of Police that the Queen of England no longer rules Port Burdock. The Invisible Man is the new ruler. It is day one of the Reign of the Invisible Man the First.

I will start my rule with an execution as an example to others who might try to conspire against me. That execution will be of a man named Kemp. He may lock himself away or hide or surround himself with guards or put on armor, but I swear that Death will come! Do not help Kemp, any of you, or Death will come to you too! Today is Kemp's day to die!"

Kemp immediately rang for his housekeeper and instructed her to be sure all the windows were locked and the shutters closed. He went upstairs and checked his study windows himself, then took a little revolver out of a locked drawer. After making certain that it was loaded, he put it into the pocket of his

Taking Out a Revolver

lounging jacket, then returned to his lunch, his mind racing as he ate.

Finally, he struck the table with his fists and shouted, "By Heavens, we *will* catch him! And *I* will be the bait."

Kemp jumped up from the table and went to his desk, where he wrote a short note. He again called his housekeeper and told her, "Take this to Colonel Adye as quickly as you can. Stay at the police station until I come for you. There's a madman after me, but you will be safe there."

Less than an hour later, the front door bell rang and Kemp went downstairs to answer it. He unbolted the door, but left the chain fastened, opening it just a few inches. He didn't show himself until he heard Colonel Adye's voice.

"Open up, Kemp! Quickly! There's trouble! Your housekeeper's been attacked."

"Oh, no!" cried the doctor as he released the chain. "Is she all right?"

"There's a Madman After Me!"

"She's down at the station in hysterics. Said she was delivering a note to me and it was snatched out of her hand. What was it?"

"What a fool I was! It's only an hour's walk from Hintondean. He's here already!"

"What's Hintondean got to do with this?"

"Here's what." And Kemp thrust the Invisible Man's letter into Adye's hand. "Here I was, proposing we set a trap for him, and he intercepted the note and knows my plan."

"He won't risk coming here."

"Oh, yes he wi—"

At that moment, a resounding smash of glass came from upstairs. "It's my study window!" cried Kemp. "Come on!"

The men took the stairs two at a time as the smashing of glass continued. When they burst into the study, they found the room littered with splintered glass from all three windows.

"He has begun!" cried Kemp.

"There's no way he could have climbed up here. This room's on the third floor."

Splintered Glass

"But he has, and—"

Just then, the smashing of wooden boards came from downstairs.

"He's at the bedroom windows now, confound him!" cursed Kemp. "He's going to try to smash in the whole house. But he's a fool. With the inside shutters closed, the glass will fall outside and he'll cut his feet."

As the windows continued to be smashed, Adye suggested, "I'll go for the bloodhounds and be back in ten minutes. Lend me your revolver and stay locked up in here."

Kemp handed over his gun and led the Colonel to the door. As he silently slid the bolt open, he whispered, "Step out quickly, so he doesn't manage to slip inside."

No sooner was Adye out on the doorstep than Kemp slid the bolt shut and breathed a sigh of relief.

Colonel Adye marched firmly down the steps and across the lawn. As he approached the gate, a little breeze seemed to ripple the

Marching Firmly Down the Steps

grass and a voice called to him, "Stop!"

Adye stopped, but his hand tightened on the revolver in his pocket. "What is it?" he asked, trying to sound confident and brave.

"Go back in the house," said the voice.

"Sorry, I have business to take care of."

"What business?"

"That is no concern of yours!"

No sooner were the words out of his mouth than Adye felt an arm wrap around his neck and a knee thrust into his back. The next moment, he was sprawled on the ground. He pulled the revolver out of his pocket and fired wildly. But he was struck in the mouth and the revolver torn out of his hand.

Adye saw the revolver hanging in midair six feet above his head and heard the Voice snarl, "I'd kill you now if it wasn't a waste of a bullet! Now get up!"

Adye stood up. He had no desire to see his life end on this sunny June day.

"I have no quarrel with you," said the Invis-

The Revolver Hanging in Mid-Air

ible Man, "but I can't let you go back to town and get help. Go back inside now."

"Kemp won't let me in."

"You'll have to persuade him to. You have no choice."

"At least promise not to kill him."

"I promise nothing!"

While this conversation was taking place, Dr. Kemp was crouching amid the broken glass and peering out over the window sill of his study. "Why is Adye standing there talking? Why doesn't he fire?" Then a flash of sunlight reflected off the shiny revolver, and Kemp realized who was holding it now.

Just then, Adye turned towards the house, walking slowly with his hands over his head. He was followed by a little black revolver hanging in midair just inches behind him.

Suddenly, Adye leaped backwards, swung around, and made a grab for the revolver. But he missed it. The next moment, a little puff of blue smoke filled the air. Adye clutched at his

Blue Smoke Filled the Air.

chest, then fell forward on the ground and lay motionless.

Kemp remained just as motionless at the window, though his eyes were scanning the lawn and the road for a glimpse of the revolver. But it had vanished. The only movement on the road came from two policemen heading towards his house.

Just then, the house began resounding with heavy blows and the splintering of wood from the ground floor. Kemp hurried downstairs and into the kitchen, where he stood aghast. The window glass had been smashed, and the shutters had been driven in with an axe. That axe was now crashing against the iron bars of the window frame.

Kemp backed out of the kitchen into the hallway to think. The Invisible Man would be in the house in minutes, and none of the inside doors were strong enough to stop him.

The ringing of the bell startled Kemp. He ran to the front door and put up the chain, but

Hurrying Into the Kitchen

released it when the two policemen identified themselves.

"The Invisible Man's here!" cried Kemp. "And he's got an axe and a revolver!"

More resounding blows from the kitchen reached their ears. "He'll be in here any minute!" yelled Kemp, now in a panic.

He led the policemen to the dining room, where he handed them pokers from the fireplace just as a revolver and an axe appeared in midair at the doorway from the kitchen.

One poker stopped a blow from the axe, but not a shot from the revolver. The second poker came down hard on the little revolver, sending it rattling to the floor.

The axe backed away into the hall, still in the air, but now only two feet above the floor. The breathless voice of the Invisible Man gasped to the policemen, "Stand back, you two. It's Kemp I want."

"But it's *you* we want," snapped the first policeman, swinging his poker in the direction

A Revolver and an Axe

the voice was coming from.

The axe fell back, but swung again, crashing into the policeman's helmet and knocking him out.

The second policeman aimed his poker behind the axe and hit something soft. There was a sharp cry of pain, and the axe fell. The policeman swung the poker at the same spot, but hit nothing. He stepped down hard on the axe and struck again. And again he hit nothing. Then he stood still, listening for the slightest movement. There was none.

The first policeman sat up at that moment. Blood was running down his face from a cut on his head. "Where is he?" he asked.

"I hit him, but I don't know where he is. He must have slipped out of the house. See, the dining room window's open, and our *brave* Dr. Kemp must have slipped out through it too. Some hero he turned out to be!"

The Axe Swung Again

Banging at the Door!

Chapter 18

Visible in Death

When Arthur Kemp climbed out the dining room window, he ran across his vegetable garden towards a path leading to a clump of trees. The asparagus that his boots trampled were trampled again minutes later by invisible feet following him.

Kemp ran towards the house of his nearest neighbor, but his shouts and banging at the door were of no use. Fear of the Invisible Man kept that door locked to him.

Though his face was white, Kemp kept his wits about him as he ran towards town. He deliberately traveled on rough ground and over the broken glass that had been spread on the road. He knew only too well what would happen when invisible bare feet ran over that same road.

As he entered Port Burdock, Kemp heard footsteps gaining on him. His own heavy breathing was echoed by unseen breathing close behind.

"The Invisible Man!" he cried to the road workers and to the people boarding the tram at the edge of town. "He's behind me!"

The crowd scattered. Women and children rushed indoors. Road workers lifted their picks and shovels and began running along with him to help.

Suddenly, Kemp stopped and shouted to them, "Form a line across the ro—"

But at that moment, he was hit hard under the ear. He reeled, but managed to keep his balance as he swung his fist at his invisible opponent. Then he was hit again under the jaw,

"He's Behind Me!"

and he sprawled headlong on the ground. The next moment, an invisible knee was pressing into his chest and powerful fingers were gripping his throat.

Just as Kemp was trying to loosen the Invisible Man's grasp, the spade of one of the road workers came whirling through the air above him and struck something with a dull thud. The grip on Kemp's neck loosened, and the doctor felt a drop of something wet fall onto his face.

He managed to roll out from under the weight that lay on top of him and roll over, pinning an invisible body to the ground.

"Help!" he called. "I've got him. Someone hold his feet!"

Men rushed into the struggle from all sides, making the pile-up look like a football play. Fists were flying and legs were kicking until wild screams of "Mercy! Have mercy!" came from beneath the pileup.

"Get back, you fools!" cried Kemp through

Men Rushed From All Sides

bleeding, swollen lips as he shoved men off the invisible body. "He's hurt."

The men moved back, only to see the doctor kneeling in the air while holding invisible arms pinned to the ground.

"Don't let go of him!" cried one man. "He's probably faking being hurt."

"He's not faking," said Kemp angrily.

Kemp lifted one hand from the Invisible Man's arms and felt around for the man's face. "His mouth's all wet," he said. "It feels like blood." Then he moved his hand down to where the man's chest would be. "Oh, God! He's not breathing. I can't feel his heart and—"

"Look there!" cried an old woman in the crowd as she pointed down.

All eyes followed her wrinkled finger to the outline of a hand that seemed to be as transparent as glass, with veins, arteries, bones, and nerves showing. Even as the crowd stared in amazement, the hand seemed to change from transparent to cloudy.

Transparent as Glass

"And look there!" gasped a man. "Here's his feet a-showin' too."

And so, slowly, beginning at his hands and feet and creeping along to the center of his body, the strange change continued. First came the nerves, then the bones and arteries, the organs, and the flesh and skin. The man's crushed chest was now visible.

Kemp took off his jacket to cover the naked body of 30-year-old Jack Griffin.

"Cover his face too!" cried a woman when she saw the gaping eyes and the twisted, angry mouth.

Someone brought out a sheet from the Jolly Cricketer and covered Griffin from head to toe. Then Arthur Kemp gently lifted the bruised and broken body of his old school mate and carried it into the inn.

"Cover His Face, Too!"

A Wealthy Inkeeper

Chapter 19

The Stolen Notebooks

The tale of the strange and evil experiment of the Invisible Man is ended. But if you want to learn more about him, go to the Invisible Man Inn near Port Stowe and talk to the wealthy innkeeper—a short, stout little man who no longer wears a ragged coat tied with twine or a furry silk top hat.

Buy some food from him and you'll hear the story of his adventures with the Invisible Man and how he outwitted the lawyers who tried to take away the money that the police found in his pockets.

But if you ask him what became of the three notebooks, he'll swear that it was the Invisible Man himself who took them and hid them, and that it was Dr. Kemp who accused him, Mr. Thomas Marvel, of stealing them and hiding them somewhere.

But on Sundays, when the inn is closed, Marvel goes into his parlor, bolts the door, and pulls down the blinds. Then he unlocks the cupboard and takes out a box. He unlocks that box and takes out three notebooks.

Marvel sits down in his armchair, lights his pipe, and reads the coded symbols on the pages before him. "X, a little 2 up in the air, a cross . . . and a fiddle-de-dee. What wonderful secrets are in here! Once I get to understand 'em, I'll just . . . well, I wouldn't do what *he* did, that's for sure."

And though Kemp and Adye have questioned him, no one but Thomas Marvel knows where the Invisible Man's secret notebooks are . . . and no one will know until Marvel dies. . . .

Reading the Coded Symbols